Samuel Beckett was born in Dublin in 1906. During the 1920s he went to live in Paris, and was a close friend of James Joyce who regarded him as a very promising writer. He published novels, stories and poems, but did not achieve fame until his play, *Waiting for Godot*, was performed in 1953. Since then he has gained recognition as perhaps the greatest living prose writer, a magnificent novelist as well as playwright. His novels include *Murphy* (1938), *Watt* (1944), and the trilogy, *Molloy*, *Malone Dies* and *The Unnamable* (1959). Among his plays are *End Game* (1957) and *Krapp's Last Tape* (1959). He writes with equal ease in French and English, though his most recent books have been written originally in French. Beckett won the Prix Formentor in 1961 for his outstanding contribution to world literature, and the Nobel Prize for Literature in 1969.

Samuel Beckett

COMPANY

published by Pan Books

First published in Great Britain 1980 by John Calder (Publishers) Ltd
This Picador edition published 1982 by Pan Books Ltd,
Cavaye Place, London SW10 9PG
Part of this text first appeared in *New Writing and Writers 17* under the title
'Heard in the Dark' and a further section appeared in *Journal of Beckett Studies 5*
under the title of 'Heard in the Dark 2'.
© Samuel Beckett 1979, 1980
· ISBN 0 330 26709 4
Printed and bound in Great Britain by
Richard Clay (The Chaucer Press) Ltd, Bungay, Suffolk

COMPANY

A VOICE comes to one in the dark. Imagine.

To one on his back in the dark. This he can tell by the pressure on his hind parts and by how the dark changes when he shuts his eyes and again when he opens them again. Only a small part of what is said can be verified. As for example when he hears, You are on your back in the dark. Then he must acknowledge the truth of what is said. But by far the greater part of what is said cannot be verified. As for example when he hears, You first saw the light on such and such a day. Sometimes the two are combined as for example, You first saw the light on such and such a day and now you are on your back in the dark. A device perhaps from the incontrovertibility of the one to win credence for the other. That then is the proposition. To one on his back in the dark a voice tells of a past. With occasional allusion to a present and more rarely to a future as for example, You will end as you now are. And in another dark or in the same another devising it all for company. Quick leave him.

Use of the second person marks the voice. That of the third that cankerous other. Could he speak to and of whom the voice speaks there would be a first. But he cannot. He shall not. You cannot. You shall not.

Apart from the voice and the faint sound of his breath there is no sound. None at least that he can hear. This he can tell by the faint sound of his breath.

Though now even less than ever given to wonder he cannot but sometimes wonder if it is indeed to and of him the voice is speaking. May not there be another with him in the dark

9

to and of whom the voice is speaking? Is he not perhaps overhearing a communication not intended for him? If he is alone on his back in the dark why does the voice not say so? Why does it never say for example, You saw the light on such and such a day and now you are alone on your back in the dark? Why? Perhaps for no other reason than to kindle in his mind this faint uncertainty and embarrassment.

Your mind never active at any time is now even less than ever so. This is the type of assertion he does not question. You saw the light on such and such a day and your mind never active at any time is now even less than ever so. Yet a certain activity of mind however slight is a necessary complement of company. That is why the voice does not say, You are on your back in the dark and have no mental activity of any kind. The voice alone is company but not enough. Its effect on the hearer is a necessary complement. Were it only to kindle in his mind the state of faint uncertainty and embarrassment mentioned above. But company apart this effect is clearly necessary. For were he merely to hear the voice and it to have no more effect on him than speech in Bantu or in Erse then might it not as well cease? Unless its object be by mere

11

sound to plague one in need of silence. Or of course unless as above surmised directed at another.

A small boy you come out of Connolly's Stores holding your mother by the hand. You turn right and advance in silence southward along the highway. After some hundred paces you head inland and broach the long steep homeward. You make ground in silence hand in hand through the warm still summer air. It is late afternoon and after some hundred paces the sun appears above the crest of the rise. Looking up at the blue sky and then at your mother's face you break the silence asking her if it is not in reality much more distant than it appears. The sky that is. The blue sky. Receiving no answer you mentally reframe your question and some hundred paces later look up at her face again and ask her if it does not appear much less distant than in reality it is. For some reason you could never fathom this question must have angered her exceedingly. For she shook off your little hand and made you a cutting retort you have never forgotten.

If the voice is not speaking to him it must be speaking to another. So with what reason remains he reasons. To another of that other. Or of him.

Or of another still. To another of that other or of him or of another still. To one on his back in the dark in any case. Of one on his back in the dark whether the same or another. So with what reason remains he reasons and reasons ill. For were the voice speaking not to him but to another then it must be of that other it is speaking and not of him or of another still. Since it speaks in the second person. Were it not of him to whom it is speaking speaking but of another it would not speak in the second person but in the third. For example, He first saw the light on such and such a day and now he is on his back in the dark. It is clear therefore that if it is not to him the voice is speaking but to another it is not of him either but of that other and none other to that other. So with what reason remains he reasons ill. In order to be company he must display a certain mental activity. But it need not be of a high order. Indeed it might be argued the lower the better. Up to a point. The lower the order of mental activity the better the company. Up to a point.

You first saw the light in the room you most likely were conceived in. The big bow window looked west to the mountains. Mainly west. For being bow it looked also a little south and a little north. Necessarily. A little south to more mountain and a little north to foothill and plain. The mid-wife was none other than a Dr Hadden or Haddon. Straggling grey moustache and hunted look. It being a public holiday your father left the house soon after his breakfast with a flask and a package of his favourite egg sandwiches for a tramp in the mountains. There was nothing unusual in this. But on that particular morning his love of walking and wild scenery was not the only mover. But he was moved also to take himself off and out of the way by his aversion to the pains and general unpleasantness of labour and delivery. Hence the sandwiches which he relished at noon

16

looking out to sea from the lee of a great rock on the first summit scaled. You may imagine his thoughts before and after as he strode through the gorse and heather. When he returned at nightfall he learned to his dismay from the maid at the back door that labour was still in swing. Despite its having begun before he left the house full ten hours earlier. He at once hastened to the coachhouse some twenty yards distant where he housed his De Dion Bouton. He shut the doors behind him and climbed into the driver's seat. You may imagine his thoughts as he sat there in the dark not knowing what to think. Though footsore and weary he was on the point of setting out anew across the fields in the young moonlight when the maid came running to tell him it was over at last. Over!

You are an old man plodding along a narrow country road. You have been out since break of day and now it is evening. Sole sound in the silence your footfalls. Rather sole sounds for they vary from one to the next. You listen to each one and add it in your mind to the growing sum of those that went before. You halt with bowed head on the verge of the ditch and convert into yards. On the basis now of two steps per yard. So many since dawn to add to yesterday's. To yesteryear's. To yesteryears'. Days other than today and so akin. The giant tot in miles. In leagues. How often round the earth already. Halted too at your elbow during these computations your father's shade. In his old tramping rags. Finally on side by side from nought anew.

The voice comes to him now from one quarter and now from another. Now faint from afar and now a murmur in his ear. In the course of a single sentence it may change place and tone. Thus for example clear from above his upturned face, You first saw the light at Easter and now. Then a murmur in his ear, You are on your

back in the dark. Or of course vice
versa. Another trait its long silences
when he dare almost hope it is at an
end. Thus to take the same example
clear from above his upturned face,
You first saw the light of day the day
Christ died and now. Then long after
on his nascent hope the murmur, You
are on your back in the dark. Or of
course vice versa.

Another trait its repetitiousness.
Repeatedly with only minor variants
the same bygone. As if willing him
by this dint to make it his. To confess,
Yes I remember. Perhaps even to
have a voice. To murmur, Yes I
remember. What an addition to

company that would be! A voice in the first person singular. Murmuring now and then, Yes I remember.

An old beggar woman is fumbling at a big garden gate. Half blind. You know the place well. Stone deaf and not in her right mind the woman of the house is a crony of your mother. She was sure she could fly once in the air. So one day she launched herself from a first floor window. On the way home from kindergarten on your tiny cycle you see the poor old beggar woman trying to get in. You dismount and open the gate for her. She blesses you. What were her words? God reward you little master.

Some such words. God save you little master.

A faint voice at loudest. It slowly ebbs till almost out of hearing. Then slowly back to faint full. At each slow ebb hope slowly dawns that it is dying. He must know it will flow again. And yet at each slow ebb hope slowly dawns that it is dying.

Slowly he entered dark and silence and lay there for so long that with what judgement remained he judged them to be final. Till one day the voice. One day! Till in the end the voice saying, You are on your back in the dark. Those its first words.

Long pause for him to believe his ears and then from another quarter the same. Next the vow not to cease till hearing cease. You are on your back in the dark and not till hearing cease will this voice cease. Or another way. As in shadow he lay and only the odd sound slowly silence fell and darkness gathered. That were perhaps better company. For what odd sound? Whence the shadowy light?

You stand at the tip of the high board. High above the sea. In it your father's upturned face. Upturned to you. You look down to the loved trusted face. He calls to you to jump. He calls, Be a brave boy. The red round face. The thick moustache. The greying hair. The swell sways it under and sways it up again. The far call again, Be a brave boy. Many eyes upon you. From the water and from the bathing place.

The odd sound. What a mercy to have that to turn to. Now and then. In dark and silence to close as if to light the eyes and hear a sound. Some object moving from its place to its last place. Some soft thing softly stirring soon to stir no more. To darkness visible to close the eyes and hear if only that. Some soft thing softly stirring soon to stir no more.

By the voice a faint light is shed. Dark lightens while it sounds. Deepens when it ebbs. Lightens with flow back to faint full. Is whole again when it ceases. You are on your back in the dark. Had the eyes been open then they would have marked a change.

Whence the shadowy light? What company in the dark! To close the eyes and try to imagine that. Whence once the shadowy light. No source. As if faintly luminous all his little void. What can he have seen then above his upturned face. To close the eyes in the dark and try to imagine that.

Another trait the flat tone. No life. Same flat tone at all times. For its affirmations. For its negations. For its interrogations. For its exclamations. For its imperations. Same flat tone. You were once. You were never. Were you ever? Oh never to have been! Be again. Same flat tone.

Can he move? Does he move? Should he move? What a help that would be. When the voice fails. Some movement however small. Were it but of a hand closing. Or opening if closed to begin. What a help that would be in the dark! To close the eyes and see that hand. Palm upward filling the whole field. The lines. The fingers slowly down. Or up if down to begin. The lines of that old palm.

There is of course the eye. Filling the whole field. The hood slowly down. Or up if down to begin. The globe. All pupil. Staring up. Hooded. Bared. Hooded again. Bared again.

If he were to utter after all? However feebly. What an addition to company that would be! You are on your back in the dark and one day you will utter again. One day! In the end. In the end you will utter again. Yes I remember. That was I. That was I then.

You are alone in the garden. Your mother is in the kitchen making ready for afternoon tea with Mrs Coote. Making the wafer-thin bread and butter. From behind a bush you watch Mrs Coote arrive. A small thin sour woman. Your mother answers her saying, He is playing in the garden. You climb to near the top of a great fir. You sit a little listening to all the sounds. Then throw yourself off. The great boughs break your fall. The needles. You lie a little with your face to the ground. Then climb the tree again. Your mother answers Mrs Coote again saying, He has been a very naughty boy.

What with what feeling remains does he feel about now as compared to then? When with what judgement remained he judged his condition final. As well inquire what he felt then about then as compared to before. When he still moved or tarried in remains of light. As then there was no then so there is none now.

In another dark or in the same another devising it all for company. This at first sight seems clear. But as the eye dwells it grows obscure. Indeed the longer the eye dwells the obscurer it grows. Till the eye closes and freed from pore the mind inquires, What does this mean? What finally does this mean that at first sight seemed clear? Till it the mind too closes as it were. As the window might close of a dark empty room. The single window giving on outer dark. Then nothing more. No. Unhappily no. Pangs of faint light and stirrings still. Unformulable gropings of the mind. Unstillable.

Nowhere in particular on the way from A to Z. Or say for verisimilitude the Ballyogan Road. That dear old back road. Somewhere on the Ballyogan Road in lieu of nowhere in particular. Where no truck any more. Somewhere on the Ballyogan Road on the way from A to Z. Head sunk totting up the tally on the verge of the ditch. Foothills to left. Croker's Acres ahead. Father's shade to right and a little to the rear. So many times already round the earth. Topcoat once green stiff with age and grime from chin to insteps. Battered once buff block hat and quarter boots still a match. No other garments if any to be seen. Out since break of day and night now falling. Reckoning ended on together from nought anew. As if bound for Stepaside. When suddenly you cut through the hedge and vanish hobbling east across the gallops.

For why or? Why in another dark

or in the same? And whose voice asking this? Who asks, Whose voice asking this? And answers, His soever who devises it all. In the same dark as his creature or in another. For company. Who asks in the end, Who asks? And in the end answers as above? And adds long after to himself, Unless another still. Nowhere to be found. Nowhere to be sought. The unthinkable last of all. Unnamable. Last person. I. Quick leave him.

The light there was then. On your back in the dark the light there was then. Sunless cloudless brightness. You slip away at break of day and climb to your hiding place on the hillside.

A nook in the gorse. East beyond the sea the faint shape of high mountain. Seventy miles away according to your Longman. For the third or fourth time in your life. The first time you told them and were derided. All you had seen was cloud. So now you hoard it in your heart with the rest. Back home at nightfall supperless to bed. You lie in the dark and are back in that light. Straining out from your nest in the gorse with your eyes across the water till they ache. You close them while you count a hundred. Then open and strain again. Again and again. Till in the end it is there. Palest blue against the pale sky. You lie in the dark and are back in that light. Fall asleep in that sunless cloud-less light. Sleep till morning light.

Deviser of the voice and of its hearer and of himself. Deviser of himself for company. Leave it at that. He speaks of himself as of another. He says speaking of himself, He speaks of himself as of another. Himself he devises too for company. Leave it at that. Confusion too is company up to a point. Better hope deferred than none. Up to a point. Till the heart starts to sicken. Company too up to a point. Better a sick heart than none. Till it starts to break. So speaking of himself he concludes for the time being, For the time being leave it at that.

In the same dark as his creature or in another not yet imagined. Nor in what position. Whether standing or sitting or lying or in some other position in the dark. These are among the matters yet to be imagined. Matters of which as yet no inkling. The test is company. Which of the two darks is the better company. Which of all imaginable positions has the most to offer in the way of company. And similarly for the other matters yet to be imagined. Such as if such decisions irreversible. Let him for example after due imagination decide in favour of the supine position or prone and this in practice prove less companionable than anticipated.

May he then or may he not replace it by another? Such as huddled with his legs drawn up within the semi-circle of his arms and his head on his knees. Or in motion. Crawling on all fours. Another in another dark or in the same crawling on all fours devising it all for company. Or some other form of motion. The possible encounters. A dead rat. What an addition to company that would be! A rat long dead.

Might not the hearer be improved? Made more companionable if not downright human. Mentally perhaps there is room for enlivenment. An attempt at reflexion at least. At recall.

At speech even. Conation of some kind however feeble. A trace of emotion. Signs of distress. A sense of failure. Without loss of character. Delicate ground. But physically? Must he lie inert to the end? Only the eyelids stirring on and off since technically they must. To let in and shut out the dark. Might he not cross his feet? On and off. Now left on right and now a little later the reverse. No. Quite out of keeping. He lie with crossed feet? One glance dispels. Some movement of the hands? A hand. A clenching and unclenching. Difficult to justify. Or raised to brush away a fly. But there are no flies. Then why not let there be? The temptation is great. Let there be a fly. For him to brush away. A live fly mistaking him for dead. Made aware of its error and renewing it incontinent. What an addition to company that would be! A live fly mistaking him for dead. But no. He would not brush away a fly.

You take pity on a hedgehog out in the cold and put it in an old hatbox with some worms. This box with the hog inside you then place in a disused hutch wedging the door open for the poor creature to come and go at will. To go in search of food and having eaten to regain the warmth and security of its box in the hutch. There then is the hedgehog in its box in the hutch with enough worms to tide it over. A last look to make sure all is as it should be before taking yourself off to look for something else to pass the time heavy already on your hands at that tender age. The glow at your good deed is slower than usual to cool and fade. You glowed readily in those days but seldom for long. Hardly had the glow been kindled by some good deed on your part or by some little triumph over your rivals or by a word of praise from your parents or mentors when it would begin to cool and fade leaving you in a very short time as chill and dim as before. Even in those days. But not this day. It was on an autumn afternoon you found the hedgehog and took pity on it in the way described and you were still the better for it when your bedtime came. Kneeling at your bedside you included it the hedgehog in your detailed prayer to God to bless all you loved. And tossing in your warm bed waiting for sleep to come you were still faintly glowing at the thought of what a fortunate hedgehog it was to have crossed your path as it did. A narrow clay path edged with sere box edging. As you stood there wondering how best to pass the time till bedtime it parted the edging on the one side and was making straight for the edging on the other when you entered its life. Now the next morning not only was the glow spent but a great uneasiness had taken its place. A suspicion that all was perhaps not as it should be. That rather than do as you did you had perhaps better let good alone and the hedgehog pursue its way. Days if not weeks passed before you could bring yourself to return to the hutch. You have never forgotten what you found then. You are on your back in the dark and have never forgotten what you found then. The mush. The stench.

Impending for some time the following. Need for company not continuous. Moments when his own unrelieved a relief. Intrusion of voice at such. Similarly image of hearer. Similarly his own. Regret then at having brought them about and problem how dispel them. Finally what meant by his own unrelieved? What possible relief? Leave it at that for the moment.

Let the hearer be named H. Aspirate. Haitch. You Haitch are on your back in the dark. And let him know his name. No longer any question of his overhearing. Of his not being meant. Though logically none in any case. Of words murmured in his ear to wonder if to him! So he is. So that faint uneasiness lost. That faint hope.

To one with so few occasions to feel. So inapt to feel. Asking nothing better in so far as he can ask anything than to feel nothing. Is it desirable? No. Would he gain thereby in companionability? No. Then let him not be named H. Let him be again as he was. The hearer. Unnamable. You.

Imagine closer the place where he lies. Within reason. To its form and dimensions a clue is given by the voice afar. Receding afar or there with abrupt saltation or resuming there after pause. From above and from all sides and levels with equal remoteness at its most remote. At no time from below. So far. Suggesting one lying on the floor of a hemispherical chamber of generous diameter with ear dead centre. How generous? Given faintness of voice at its least faint some sixty feet should suffice or thirty from ear to any given point of encompassing surface. So much for form and dimensions. And composition? What and where clue to that if any anywhere. Reserve for the moment. Basalt is tempting. Black basalt. But reserve for the moment. So he imagines to himself as voice and hearer pall. But further imagination shows him to have imagined ill. For with what right affirm of a faint sound that it is a less faint made fainter by farness and not a true faint near at hand? Or of a faint fading to fainter that it recedes and not in situ decreases. If with none then no light from the voice on the place where our old hearer lies. In immeasurable dark. Contourless. Leave it at that for the moment. Adding only, What kind of imagination is this so reason-ridden? A kind of its own.

Another devising it all for company. In the same dark as his creature or in another. Quick imagine. The same.

Might not the voice be improved? Made more companionable. Say changing now for some time past though no tense in the dark in that dim mind. All at once over and in train and to come. But for the other say for some time past some improvement. Same flat tone as initially imagined and same repetitiousness. No improving those. But less mobility. Less variety of faintness. As if seeking optimum position. From which to discharge with greatest effect. The ideal amplitude for effortless audition. Neither offending the ear with loudness nor through converse excess constraining it to strain. How far more companionable such an organ than it initially in haste imagined. How far more likely to achieve its object. To have the hearer have a past and acknowledge it. You were born on an

Easter Friday after long labour. Yes I remember. The sun had not long sunk behind the larches. Yes I remember. As best to erode the drop must strike unwavering. Upon the place beneath.

The last time you went out the snow lay on the ground. You now on your back in the dark stand that morning on the sill having pulled the door gently to behind you. You lean back against the door with bowed head making ready to set out. By the time you open your eyes your feet have disappeared and the skirts of your greatcoat come to rest on the surface of the snow. The dark scene seems lit from below. You see yourself at that last outset leaning against the door with closed eyes waiting for the word from you to go. To be gone. Then the snowlit scene. You lie in the dark with closed eyes and see yourself there as described making ready to strike out and away across the expanse of light. You hear again the click of the door pulled gently to and the silence before the steps can start. Next thing you are on your way across the white pasture afrolic with lambs in spring and strewn with red placentae. You take the course you always take which is a beeline for the gap or ragged point in the quickset that forms the western fringe. Thither from your entering the pasture you need

normally from eighteen hundred to
two thousand paces depending on
your humour and the state of the
ground. But on this last morning
many more will be required. Many
many more. The beeline is so familiar
to your feet that if necessary they
could keep to it and you sightless with
error on arrival of not more than a
few feet north or south. And indeed
without any such necessity unless
from within this is what they normally
do and not only here. For you advance
if not with closed eyes though this as
often as not at least with them fixed
on the momentary ground before
your feet. That is all of nature you
have seen. Since finally you bowed

your head. The fleeting ground before your feet. From time to time. You do not count your steps any more. For the simple reason they number each day the same. Average day in day out the same. The way being always the same. You keep count of the days and every tenth day multiply. And add. Your father's shade is not with you any more. It fell out long ago. You do not hear your footfalls any more. Unhearing unseeing you go your way. Day after day. The same way. As if there were no other any more. For you there is no other any more. You used never to halt except to make your reckoning. So as to plod on from nought anew. This need removed as

we have seen there is none in theory to
halt any more. Save perhaps a moment
at the outermost point. To gather
yourself together for the return. And
yet you do. As never before. Not for
tiredness. You are no more tired now
than you always were. Not because of
age. You are no older now than you
always were. And yet you halt as
never before. So that the same hundred
yards you used to cover in a matter of
three to four minutes may now take
you anything from fifteen to twenty.
The foot falls unbidden in midstep or
next for lift cleaves to the ground
bringing the body to a stand. Then a
speechlessness whereof the gist, Can
they go on? Or better, Shall they go

on? The barest gist. Stilled when finally as always hitherto they do. You lie in the dark with closed eyes and see the scene. As you could not at the time. The dark cope of sky. The dazzling land. You at a standstill in the midst. The quarter boots sunk to the tops. The skirts of the greatcoat resting on the snow. In the old bowed head in the old block hat speechless misgiving. Halfway across the pasture on your beeline to the gap. The unerring feet fast. You look behind you as you could not then and see their trail. A great swerve. Withershins. Almost as if all at once the heart too heavy. In the end too heavy.

Bloom of adulthood. Imagine a whiff of that. On your back in the dark you remember. Ah you you remember. Cloudless May day. She joins you in the little summerhouse. A rustic hexahedron. Entirely of logs. Both larch and fir. Six feet across. Eight from floor to vertex. Area twenty-four square feet to furthest decimal. Two small multicoloured lights vis-à-vis. Small stained diamond panes. Under each a ledge. There on summer Sundays after his midday meal your father loved to retreat with Punch and a cushion. The waist of his trousers unbuttoned he sat on the one ledge turning the pages. You on the other with your feet dangling. When he chuckled you tried to chuckle too. When his chuckle died yours too. That you should try to imitate his chuckle pleased and tickled him greatly and sometimes he would chuckle for no other reason than to hear you try to chuckle too. Sometimes you turn your head and look out through a rose-red pane. You press your little nose against the pane and all without is rosy. The years have flown and there at the same place as then you sit in the bloom of adulthood bathed in rainbow light gazing before you. She is late. You close your eyes and try to calculate the volume. Simple sums you find a help in times of trouble. A haven. You arrive in the end at seven cubic yards approximately. Even still in the timeless dark you find figures a comfort. You assume a certain heart rate and reckon how many thumps a day. A week. A month. A year. And assuming a certain lifetime a lifetime. Till the last thump. But for the moment with hardly more than seventy American billion behind you you sit in the little summerhouse working out the volume. Seven cubic yards approximately. This strikes you for some reason as improbable and you set about your sum anew. But you have not made much headway when her light step is heard. Light for a woman of her size. You open with quickening

55

pulse your eyes and a moment later that seems an eternity her face appears at the window. Mainly blue in this position the natural pallor you so admire as indeed from it no doubt wholly blue your own. For natural pallor is a property you have in common. The violet lips do not return your smile. Now this window being flush with your eyes from where you sit and the floor as near as no matter with the outer ground you cannot but wonder if she has not sunk to her knees. Knowing from experience that the height or length you have in common is the sum of equal segments. For when bolt upright or lying at full stretch you cleave face to face then your knees meet and your pubes and the hairs of your heads mingle. Does it follow from this that the loss of height for the body that sits is the same as for it that kneels? At this point assuming height of seat adjustable as in the case of certain piano stools you close your eyes the better with mental measure to measure and compare the first and second segments namely from sole to kneepad and thence to pelvic girdle. How given you were both moving and at rest to the closed eye in your waking hours! By day and by night. To that perfect dark. That shadowless light. Simply to be gone. Or for affair as now. A single leg appears. Seen from above. You separate the segments and lay them side by side. It is as you half surmised. The upper is the longer and the sitter's loss the greater when seat at knee level. You leave the pieces lying there and open your eyes to find her sitting before you. All dead still. The ruby lips do not return your smile. Your gaze descends to the breasts. You do not remember them so big. To the abdomen. Same impression. Dissolve to your father's straining against the unbuttoned waistband. Can it be she is with child without your having asked for as much as her hand? You go back into your mind. She too did you but know has closed her eyes. So you sit face to face in the little summerhouse. With eyes closed and your hands on your pubes. In that rainbow light. That dead still.

Wearied by such stretch of imagining he ceases and all ceases. Till feeling the need for company again he tells himself to call the hearer M at least. For readier reference. Himself some other character. W. Devising it all himself included for company. In the same dark as M when last heard of. In what posture and whether fixed or mobile left open. He says further to himself referring to himself, When last he referred to himself it was to say he was in the same dark as his creature.

Not in another as once seemed possible. The same. As more companionable. And that his posture there remained to be devised. And to be decided whether fast or mobile. Which of all imaginable postures least liable to pall? Which of motion or of rest the more entertaining in the long run? And in the same breath too soon to say and why after all not say without further ado what can later be unsaid and what if it could not? What then? Could he now if he chose move out of the dark he chose when last heard of and away from his creature into another? Should he now decide to lie and come later to regret it could he then rise to his feet for example and lean against a wall or pace to and fro? Could M be reimagined in an easy chair? With hands free to go to his assistance? There in the same dark as his creature he leaves himself to these perplexities while wondering as every now and then he wonders in the back of his mind if the woes of the world are all they used to be. In his day.

M so far as follows. On his back in a dark place form and dimensions yet to be devised. Hearing on and off a voice of which uncertain whether addressed to him or to another sharing his situation. There being nothing to show when it describes correctly his situation that the description is not for the benefit of another in the same situation. Vague distress at the vague thought of his perhaps overhearing a confidence when he hears for example, You are on your back in the dark. Doubts gradually dashed as voice from questing far and wide closes in upon him. When it ceases no other sound than his breath. When it ceases long enough vague hope it may have said its last. Mental activity of a low order. Rare flickers of reasoning of no avail. Hope and despair and suchlike barely felt. How current situation arrived at unclear. No that then to compare to this now. Only eyelids move. When for relief from outer and inner dark they close and open respectively. Other small local movements eventually within moderation not to be despaired of. But no improvement by means of such achieved so far. Or on a higher plane by such addition to company as a movement of sustained sorrow or desire or remorse or curiosity or anger and so on. Or by some successful act of intellection as were he to think to himself referring to himself, Since he cannot think he will give up trying. Is there anything to add to this esquisse? His unnamability. Even M must go. So W reminds himself of his creature as so far created. W? But W too is creature. Figment.

Yet another then. Of whom nothing. Devising figments to temper his nothingness. Quick leave him. Pause and again in panic to himself, Quick leave him.

Devised deviser devising it all for company. In the same figment dark as his figments. In what posture and if or not as hearer in his for good not yet devised. Is not one immovable enough? Why duplicate this particular solace? Then let him move. Within reason. On all fours. A moderate crawl torso well clear of the ground eyes front alert. If this no better than nothing cancel. If possible. And in the void regained another motion. Or none. Leaving only the most helpful posture to be devised. But to be going on with let him crawl. Crawl and fall. Crawl again and fall again. In the same figment dark as his other figments.

From ranging far and wide as if in quest the voice comes to rest and constant faintness. To rest where? Imagine warily.

Above the upturned face. Falling tangent to the crown. So that in the faint light it sheds were there a mouth to be seen he would not see it. Roll as he might his eyes. Height from the ground?

Arm's length. Force? Low. A mother's stooping over cradle from behind. She moves aside to let the father look. In his turn he murmurs to the newborn. Flat tone unchanged. No trace of love.

You are on your back at the foot of an aspen. In its trembling shade. She at right angles propped on her elbows head between her hands. Your eyes opened and closed have looked in hers looking in yours. In your dark you look in them again. Still. You feel on your face the fringe of her long black hair stirring in the still air. Within the tent of hair your faces are hidden from view. She murmurs, Listen to the

66

leaves. Eyes in each other's eyes you listen to the leaves. In their trembling shade.

Crawling and falling then. Crawling again and falling again. If this finally no improvement on nothing he can always fall for good. Or have never risen to his knees. Contrive how such crawl unlike the voice may serve to chart the area. However roughly. First what is the unit of crawl? Corresponding to the footstep of erect locomotion. He rises to all fours and makes ready to set out. Hands and knees angles of an oblong two foot long width irrelevant. Finally say left knee moves forward six inches thus half halving distance between it and homologous hand. Which then in due course in its turn moves forward by as much. Oblong now rhomboid. But for no longer than it takes right knee and hand to follow suit. Oblong restored. So on till he drops. Of all modes of crawl this the repent amble possibly the least common. And so possibly of all the most diverting.

So as he crawls the mute count. Grain by grain in the mind. One two three four one. Knee hand knee hand two. One foot. Till say after five he falls. Then sooner or later on from nought anew. One two three four one. Knee hand knee hand two. Six. So on.

In what he wills a beeline. Till having encountered no obstacle discouraged he heads back the way he came. From nought anew. Or in some quite different direction. In what he hopes a beeline. Till again with no dead end for his pains he renounces and embarks on yet another course. From nought anew. Well aware or little doubting how darkness may deflect. Withershins on account of the heart. Or conversely to shortest path convert deliberate veer. Be that as it may and crawl as he will no bourne as yet. As yet imaginable. Hand knee hand knee as he will. Bourneless dark.

Would it be reasonable to imagine

the hearer as mentally quite inert? Except when he hears. That is when the voice sounds. For what if not it and his breath is there for him to hear? Aha! The crawl. Does he hear the crawl? The fall? What an addition to company were he but to hear the crawl. The fall. The rising to all fours again. The crawl resumed. And wonder to himself what in the world such sounds might signify. Reserve for a duller moment. What if not sound could set his mind in motion? Sight? The temptation is strong to decree there is nothing to see. But too late for the moment. For he sees a change of dark when he opens or shuts his eyes. And he may see the faint light the voice imagined to shed. Rashly imagined. Light infinitely faint it is true since now no more than a mere murmur. Here suddenly seen how his eyes close as soon as the voice sounds. Should they happen to be open at the time. So light as let be faintest light no longer perceived than the time it takes the lid to fall. Taste? The taste in his mouth? Long since dulled. Touch? The thrust of the ground against his bones. All the way from calcaneum to bump of philogenitiveness. Might not a notion to stir ruffle his apathy? To turn on his side. On his face. For a change. Let that much of want be conceded. With attendant relief that the days are no more when he could writhe in vain. Smell? His own? Long since dulled. And a barrier to others if any. Such as might have once emitted a rat long dead. Or some other carrion. Yet to be imagined. Unless the crawler smell. Aha! The crawling creator. Might the crawling creator be reasonably imagined to smell? Even fouler than his creature. Stirring now and then to wonder that mind so lost to wonder. To wonder what in the world can be making that alien smell. Whence in the world those wafts of villainous smell. How much more companionable could his creator but smell. Could he but smell his creator. Some sixth sense? Inexplicable pre-

monition of impending ill? Yes or
no? No. Pure reason? Beyond
experience. God is love. Yes or no?
No.

Can the crawling creator crawling
in the same create dark as his creature
create while crawling? One of the
questions he put to himself as between
two crawls he lay. And if the obvious
answer were not far to seek the most
helpful was another matter. And many
crawls were necessary and the like
number of prostrations before he
could finally make up his imagination
on this score. Adding to himself
without conviction in the same breath
as always that no answer of his was

sacred. Come what might the answer he hazarded in the end was no he could not. Crawling in the dark in the way described was too serious a matter and too all-engrossing to permit of any other business were it only the conjuring of something out of nothing. For he had not only as perhaps too hastily imagined to cover the ground in this special way but rectigrade into the bargain to the best of his ability. And furthermore to count as he went adding half foot to half foot and retain in his memory the ever-changing sum of those gone before. And finally to maintain eyes and ears at a high level of alertness for any clue however small to the nature of the place to which imagination perhaps unadvisedly had consigned him. So while in the same breath deploring a fancy so reason-ridden and observing how revocable its flights he could not but answer finally no he could not. Could not conceivably create while crawling in the same create dark as his creature.

A strand. Evening. Light dying. Soon none left to die. No. No such thing then as no light. Died on to dawn and never died. You stand with your back to the wash. No sound but its. Ever fainter as it slowly ebbs. Till it slowly flows again. You lean on a long staff. Your hands rest on the knob and on them your head. Were your eyes to open they would first see far below in the last rays the skirt of your greatcoat and the uppers of your boots emerging from the sand. Then and it alone till it vanishes the shadow of the staff on the sand. Vanishes from your sight. Moonless starless night. Were your eyes to open dark would lighten.

Crawls and falls. Lies. Lies in the dark with closed eyes resting from his crawl. Recovering. Physically and from his disappointment at having crawled again in vain. Perhaps saying to himself, Why crawl at all? Why not just lie in the dark with closed eyes and give up? Give up all. Have done with all. With bootless crawl and figments comfortless. But if on occasion so disheartened it is seldom for long. For little by little as he lies the craving for company revives. In which to escape from his own. The need to hear that voice again. If only saying again, You are on your back in the dark. Or if only, You first saw the light and cried at the close of the day when in darkness Christ at the ninth hour cried and died. The need eyes closed the better to hear to see that glimmer shed. Or with adjunction of some human weakness to improve the hearer. For example an itch beyond reach of the hand or better still within while the hand immovable. An unscratchable itch. What an addition to company that would be! Or last if not least resort to ask himself what precisely he means when he speaks of himself loosely as lying. Which in other words of all the innumerable ways of lying is likely to prove in the long run the most endearing. If having crawled in the way described he falls it would normally be on his face. Indeed given the degree of his fatigue and discouragement at this point it is hard to see how he could do otherwise. But once fallen and lying on his face there is no reason why he should not turn over on one or other of his sides or on his only back and so lie should any of these three postures offer better company than any of the other three. The supine though most tempting he must finally disallow as being already supplied by the hearer. With regard to the sidelong one glance is enough to dispel them both. Leaving him with no other choice than the prone. But how prone? Prone how? How disposed the legs? The arms? The head? Prone in the dark he strains to see how best he may lie prone. How most companionably.

See hearer clearer. Which of all the ways of lying supine the least likely in the long run to pall? After long straining eyes closed prone in the dark the following. But first naked or covered? If only with a sheet. Naked. Ghostly in the voice's glimmer that bonewhite flesh for company. Head resting mainly on occipital bump aforesaid. Legs joined at attention. Feet splayed ninety degrees. Hands invisibly manacled crossed on pubis. Other details as need felt. Leave him at that for the moment.

Numb with the woes of your kind you raise none the less your head from off your hands and open your eyes. You turn on without moving from your place the light above you. Your eyes light on the watch lying beneath it. But instead of reading the hour of night they follow round and round the second hand now followed and now preceded by its shadow. Hours later it seems to you as follows. At 60 seconds and 30 seconds shadow hidden by hand. From 60 to 30 shadow precedes hand at a distance increasing from zero at 60 to maximum at 15 and thence decreasing to new zero at 30. From 30 to 60 shadow follows hand at a distance increasing from zero at 30 to maximum at 45 and thence decreasing to new zero at 60. Slant light now to dial by moving either to either side and hand hides shadow at two quite different points as for example 50 and 20. Indeed at

any two quite different points whatever depending on degree of slant.
But however great or small the slant
and more or less remote from initial
60 and 30 the new points of zero
shadow the space between the two
remains one of 30 seconds. The
shadow emerges from under hand at
any point whatever of its circuit to
follow or precede it for the space of
30 seconds. Then disappears infinitely
briefly before emerging again to
precede or follow it for the space of
30 seconds again. And so on and on.
This would seem to be the one
constant. For the very distance itself
between hand and shadow varies as
the degree of slant. But however great

or small this distance it invariably
waxes and wanes from nothing to a
maximum 15 seconds later and to
nothing again 15 seconds later again
respectively. And so on and on. This
would seem to be a second constant.
More might have been observed on
the subject of this second hand and its
shadow in their seemingly endless
parallel rotation round and round the
dial and other variables and constants
brought to light and errors if any
corrected in what had seemed so far.
But unable to continue you bow your
head back to where it was and with
closed eyes return to the woes of your
kind. Dawn finds you still in this
position. The low sun shines on you

through the eastern window and flings all along the floor your shadow and that of the lamp left lit above you. And those of other objects also.

What visions in the dark of light! Who exclaims thus? Who asks who exclaims, What visions in the shadeless dark of light and shade! Yet another still? Devising it all for company. What a further addition to company that would be! Yet another still devising it all for company. Quick leave him.

Somehow at any price to make an end when you could go out no more you sat huddled in the dark. Having

covered in your day some twenty-five
thousand leagues or roughly thrice the
girdle. And never once overstepped a
radius of one from home. Home! So
sat waiting to be purged the old
lutist cause of Dante's first quarter-
smile and now perhaps singing praises
with some section of the blest at last.
To whom here in any case farewell.
The place is windowless. When as
you sometimes do to void the fluid
you open your eyes dark lessens.
Thus you now on your back in the
dark once sat huddled there your body
having shown you it could go out no
more. Out no more to walk the little
winding back roads and interjacent
pastures now alive with flocks and

now deserted. With at your elbow for long years your father's shade in his old tramping rags and then for long years alone. Adding step after step to the ever mounting sum of those already accomplished. Halting now and then with bowed head to fix the score. Then on from nought anew. Huddled thus you find yourself imagining you are not alone while knowing full well that nothing has occurred to make this possible. The process continues none the less lapped as it were in its meaninglessness. You do not murmur in so many words, I know this doomed to fail and yet persist. No. For the first personal and a fortiori plural pronoun had never any place in your vocabulary. But without a word you view yourself to this effect as you would a stranger suffering say from Hodgkin's disease or if you prefer Percival Pott's surprised at prayer. From time to time with unexpected grace you lie. Simultaneously the various parts set out. The arms unclasp the knees. The head lifts. The legs start to straighten. The trunk tilts backward. And together these and countless others continue on their respective ways till they can go no further and together come to rest. Supine now you resume your fable where the act of lying cut it short. And persist till the converse operation cuts it short again. So in the dark now huddled and now supine you toil in vain. And just as from the former position to the latter the shift grows easier in time and more alacrious so from the latter to the former the reverse is true. Till from the occasional relief it was supineness becomes habitual and finally the rule. You now on your back in the dark shall not rise again to clasp your legs in your arms and bow down your head till it can bow down no further. But with face upturned for good labour in vain at your fable. Till finally you hear how words are coming to an end. With every inane word a little nearer to the last. And how the fable too. The fable of one with you in the dark. The fable of one fabling of one with you in the dark. And how better in the end labour lost and silence. And you as you always were.

Alone.

Samuel Beckett
**The Beckett Trilogy – Molloy, Malone Dies
and The Unnamable** £2.50

'Unmistakably a man of genius' OBSERVER

'One of the most remarkable, most original and most haunting
prose works of the century . . . concerned with the search for
identity and with the true silence which is the end of speech . . .
Beckett has seen the Gorgon's head ; but he has not been turned
to stone' TIMES LITERARY SUPPLEMENT

'The quintessential Beckett . . . folk-sharp and humorous
grotesque fantasy' PUNCH

Deirdre Bair
Samuel Beckett £4.50
a biography

Samuel Beckett has always been the most private and mysterious
of writers, despite his status in the artistic pantheon and the
award of the 1969 Nobel Prize for Literature. There have been
many critical studies, but this is the first full biography. Beckett
said he would 'neither help nor hinder' Deirdre Bair when she
approached him in 1971, proposing to write his biography. This
apparently unhelpful pronouncement came to open many doors
and uncover much previously unknown information. The result,
this masterful biography, illuminates the life of a genius.

'Impressive translation of an enigma into a man' TIME

'Profoundly moving . . . the authentic portrait of a very great
writer and a good man' GABRIEL JOSIPOVICI, LISTENER

Franz Kafka
The Trial £1.25

The story of K, a young bank official who is suddenly woken and arrested one morning without being informed of his crime. He makes attempts to 'justify himself' against unknown charges, to discover what wrong he has done, why he has been singled out. One of this century's greatest books, which explores the predicament and alienation of contemporary humanity. Newly translated for Picador by Douglas Scott and Chris Waller with scrupulous fidelity to Kafka's original tone and style.

Herbert R. Lottman
Albert Camus: A Biography £3.95

Since the tragic death in a car-crash in 1960 of Albert Camus, author, philosopher of the Absurd and comrade of Jean-Paul Sartre, the legends surrounding his brief but remarkable life have obscured the facts. Here is the first full-scale biography of Camus : a portrait not only of the man, but of the times that made him.

'A portrait of the artist, the outsider, the humanist and sceptic, simultaneously sensuous and austere, righteous and guilty, that breaks the heart' JOHN LEONARD, NEW YORK TIMES

'Herbert Lottman's life is the first to be written, either in French or in English, and it is exhaustive, a labour of love and of wonderful industry'
JOHN STURROCK, NEW YORK TIMES BOOK REVIEW

Arthur Koestler
The Ghost in the Machine £2.50

A penetrating analysis of the relationship between reason and imagination, Arthur Koestler explores the contradictions which exist between intuitive and rational thought — contradictions which can bring man to the point of self-destruction.

'This remarkable book should be studied by everyone who is concerned about man's future'
ANTHONY STORR, SUNDAY TIMES

edited by William McGuire and abridged by
Alan McGlashan
The Freud/Jung Letters £2.50

William McGuire's collection of *The Freud/Jung Letters* is highly
regarded as a work of scholarship and is standard reading for
any serious student of psychology.

Alan McGlashan's specially commissioned abridgement brings
out the essence of this correspondence – the reflection of a
relationship of crucial importance in the history of ideas in our
century.

Doris Lessing
The Memoirs of a Survivor £1.95

'The predominating theme of the wearing away of the thin surface
of civilization is so intensely graphic in its realism that we can
come back to it convinced once again after each flight of fantasy'
FINANCIAL TIMES

'An extraordinary and compelling meditation about the enduring
need for loyalty, love and responsibility in an unprecedented time
that places unbearable demands upon people' TIME

'Her most remarkable book, the one which shows her mind at
its most extended, original and astonishing'
RONALD BRYDEN, NEW STATESMAN

Italo Calvino
If on a Winter's Night a Traveller £2.50

A fiction about fictions, a novel about novels, a book about
books. Its chief protagonists are its author and his reader. Its
progress traces the reading of a novel and the consummation of a
love affair. In its course a whole shelf of novels are begun and –
for reasons at the time entirely reasonable – never finished. Its
characters are the myriads of beings involved with the process of
creation, construction and consumption of The Book.

'I can think of no finer writer to have beside me while Italy
explodes, while Britain burns, while the world ends'
SALMAN RUSHDIE, LONDON REVIEW OF BOOKS

Josef Skvorecky
The Bass Saxophone £1.25

Two novellas by the distinguished Czech exile which evoke with
poignant irony and dark fantasy the everyday life lived under
totalitarianism — whether Nazi or Communist. Skvorecky
introduces the stories with a brilliant personal memoir of jazz, in
Czechoslovakia a persistent and enduring voice of freedom under
two tyrannies. A triumphant celebration of the beleaguered
individual's resistance to drab uniformity and spiritual meanness.

'Gave me enormous pleasure . . . of all Skvorecky's remarkable
works, these two are my favourites' GRAHAM GREENE

Ian McEwan
The Cement Garden £1.25

'In many ways a shocking book, morbid, full of repellant
imagery — and irresistibly readable . . . the effect achieved by
McEwan's quiet, precise and sensuous touch is that of magic
realism' NEW YORK REVIEW OF BOOKS

'A little masterpiece of appalling fascination' DAILY MAIL

'For a first novel, it is a darkly impressive piece of work . . . a
touch of real fictional genius' THE TIMES

'Just about perfect' SPECTATOR

Russell Hoban
Riddley Walker £1.95

'A hideously plausible picture of what our world would become,
language and all, if we went down the nuclear road to the bitter
end . . . dark parables of death and rebirth, told in a language that
attempts the impossible and achieves it'
BERNARD LEVIN, THE TIMES

'Extraordinary . . . set in a remote future and composed in an
English nobody ever spoke or wrote . . . juxtaposes pre-literate
fable and Beckettian wit, Boschian monstrosities and a hero with
Huck Finn's heart and charm, lighting by El Greco . . . a
wrenchingly vivid report on the texture of life after Doomsday'
NEW YORK TIMES BOOK REVIEW

Picador

☐	**The Beckett Trilogy**	Samuel Beckett	£2.75p
☐	**Making Love: The Picador Book of Erotic Verse**	edited by Alan Bold	£1.50p
☐	**Willard and His Bowling Trophies**	Richard Brautigan	£1.25p
☐	**Bury My Heart at Wounded Knee**	Dee Brown	£3.50p
☐	**The Price Was High, Vol. 1: The Last Uncollected Stories of F. Scott Fitzgerald**	edited by Matthew Bruccoli	£2.95p
☐	**The Road to Oxiana**	Robert Byron	£2.50p
☐	**Our Ancestors**	Italo Calvino	£3.50p
☐	**Auto Da Fé**	Elias Canetti	£2.95p
☐	**Exotic Pleasures**	Peter Carey	£1.95p
☐	**In Patagonia**	Bruce Chatwin	£1.95p
☐	**Crown Jewel**	Ralph de Boissiere	£2.75p
☐	**One Hundred Years of Solitude**	Gabriel Garcia Márquez	£2.25p
☐	**Nothing, Doting, Blindness**	Henry Green	£2.95p
☐	**The Obstacle Race**	Germaine Greer	£5.95p
☐	**Household Tales**	Brothers Grimm	£1.50p
☐	**Meetings with Remarkable Men**	Gurdjieff	£2.75p
☐	**Roots**	Alex Haley	£2.95p
☐	**Growth of the Soil**	Knut Hamsun	£2.95p
☐	**When the Tree Sings**	Stratis Haviaras	£1.95p
☐	**Dispatches**	Michael Herr	£1.75p
☐	**Riddley Walker**	Russell Hoban	£1.95p
☐	**Stories**	Desmond Hogan	£2.50p
☐	**Three Trapped Tigers**	G. Cabrera Infante	£2.95p
☐	**Unreliable Memoirs**	Clive James	£1.50p
☐	**China Men**	Maxine Hong Kingston	£1.50p
☐	**The Other Persuasion**	edited by Seymour Kleinberg	£1.75p
☐	**The Ghost in the Machine**	Arthur Koestler	£2.75p
☐	**The Memoirs of a Survivor**	Doris Lessing	£1.95p
☐	**Albert Camus**	Herbert Lottman	£3.95p
☐	**The Road to Xanadu**	John Livingston Lowes	£1.95p
☐	**The Cement Garden**	Ian McEwan	£1.50p
☐	**The Serial**	Cyra McFadden	£1.75p
☐	**McCarthy's List**	Mary Mackey	£1.95p

☐	**Short Lives**	Katinka Matson	£2.50p
☐	**The Snow Leopard**	Peter Matthiessen	£2.50p
☐	**Great Works of Jewish Fantasy**	Joachim Neugroschel	£1.95p
☐	**A Short Walk in the Hindu Kush**	Eric Newby	£1.95p
☐	**Wagner Nights**	Ernest Newman	£2.50p
☐	**The Best of Myles**	Flann O'Brien	£2.25p
☐	**Autobiography**	John Cowper Powys	£3.50p
☐	**Hadrian the Seventh**	Fr. Rolfe (Baron Corvo)	£1.25p
☐	**On Broadway**	Damon Runyon	£1.95p
☐	**Midnight's Children**	Salaman Rushdie	£2.95p
☐	**Snowblind**	Robert Sabbag	£1.95p
☐	**The Best of Saki**	Saki	£1.75p
☐	**Sanatorium under the Sign of the Hourglass**	Bruno Schultz	£1.50p
☐	**Miss Silver's Past**	Josef Skvorecky	£2.50p
☐	**Visitants**	Randolph Stow	£1.95p
☐	**Alice Fell**	Emma Tennant	£1.95p
☐	**The Flute-Player**	D. M. Thomas	£2.25p
☐	**The Great Shark Hunt**	Hunter S. Thompson	£3.25p
☐	**The Forest People**	Colin Turnbull	£1.50p
☐	**The New Tolkien Companion**	J. E. A. Tyler	£2.95p
☐	**Female Friends**	Fay Weldon	£2.50p
☐	**The Outsider**	Colin Wilson	£1.75p
☐	**The Kandy-Kolored Tangerine-Flake Streamline Baby**	Tom Wolfe	£2.25p

All these books are available at your local bookshop or newsagent, or
can be ordered direct from the publisher. Indicate the number of copies
required and fill in the form below   5

....

Name_____

(Block letters please)

Address_____

_____

Send to Pan Books (CS Department), Cavaye Place, London SW10 9PG
Please enclose remittance to the value of the cover price plus:
35p for the first book plus 15p per copy for each additional book ordered
to a maximum charge of £1.25 to cover postage and packing
Applicable only in the UK

While every effort is made to keep prices low, it is sometimes
necessary to increase prices at short notice. Pan Books reserve
the right to show on covers and charge new retail prices which
may differ from those advertised in the text or elsewhere